THE YEAR IS 119 A.Q.

AFTER QUAKE.
WHRRRRR

WHRRRRR
JAX, I CAN HEAR YOU JUST FINE --

-- WHAT DO YOU MEAN WE'RE BREAKING UP?!
YEAH. I'M ONLY SIXTEEN.
DON'T NEED TO BE SO SERIOUS.
BOTH OF YOU GUYS DISCONNECT.
JETTA, I SAID DISCONNECT! YOU'VE BEEN ON THAT HOLO CALL FOR HOURS.
I MEAN, LAYLA SAYS --
OH JAX!
LAYLA IS MY BEST FRIEND!
JAX IS A JERK.
HANG UP!
SERIOUSLY, RYKER -- I WANT EVERYONE TO PAY ATTENTION.
AND TURN OFF THAT LOUD MUSIC!
KA*KLIK
-SIGH- WHATEVER.

WARRIOR ONE

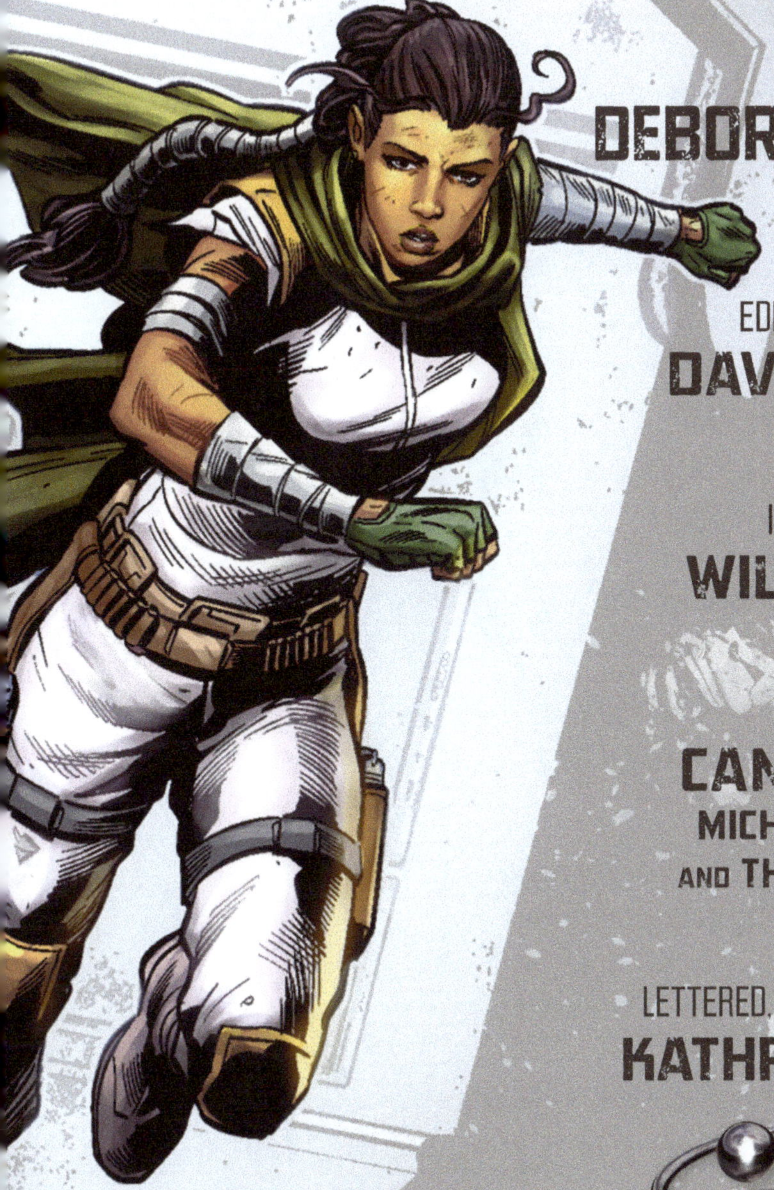

WRITTEN BY
DEBORAH M. PRATT

EDITED/ADAPTED BY
DAVID CAMPITI

ILLUSTRATED BY
WILL CONRAD

COLORED BY
CANDICE HAN,
MICHAEL BARTOLO,
AND THIAGO DAL BALLO

LETTERED, DESIGNED, AND EDITED BY
KATHRYN S. RENTA

Art Services by

WARRIOR ONE

Based on Deborah M. Pratt's
The Vision Quest world

I want to thank my cousin, Dr. Carl Bell. He was the first person to introduce me to comic books and graphic novels. Occasionally, when we visited, he would allow me to read his pristinely kept and very loved 1950s and '60s collection. I also want to thank Frank Minor for his continued support over the years.

A special thanks to my *Quantum Leap* cohorts, Deric Hughs and Benjamin Raab, for sharing their knowledge of the graphic novel world.

Most of all, I want to thank David Campiti for his Obi-Wan level patience and guidance, as well as Will Conrad, Candice Han, and Kathryn S. Renta for their stellar artistic talents. Thank you for helping bring my vision of *Warrior One* to fruition.

This is only the beginning...

~ Deborah

ISBN
978-0-9787309-2-5 (13)
9787309-2-5 (10)
2-4-6-8-10-9-7-5-3-1

HMM...?
DOOP*BE*BOOP
BWOOSH!
YOU HEARD YOUR MOTHER, RYKER.
SHUT THAT GAME DOWN!
THEN CALL HER, JAX --
-- BUT DON'T EVER CALL ME AGAIN.
EVER!

RYKER -- LOOK!
-- ATLAND CITY.
WE'LL BE THERE IN FIVE MINUTES.
WE NEVER GET INTO ATLAND CITY OR BEEN TO A WORLD'S FAIR.
YOU BOTH REALLY NEED TO BE IN THE MOMENT AND EXPERIENCE IT.
THIS IS FIRST WORLD'S FAIR EVER ON ATLANTIA? RIGHT?
TECHNICALLY, YES.
WHERE'S THE MAIN PAVILION FOR THE TOWN HALL?
RIGHT... HERE.
YOU GOT TICKETS, RIGHT?
WE'RE ON A WAITING LIST.
JETTA?
BABY?
PLEASE.
I DON'T WANT TO TALK ABOUT IT.

FINE.
THEN I WANT YOU TO DO THE MEDITATION THAT *MASTA LIA POE* TAUGHT YOU.
FIVE MINUTES.
...AHH, *FINE.*
I CAN'T LEVITATE.
UNTIL YOU BELIEVE IN YOURSELF, THAT WILL CONTINUE TO BE TRUE.
CLOSE YOUR EYES AND IMAGINE WHAT IT FEELS LIKE TO BE WEIGHTLESS.
FEEL THE HARMONIC VIBRATIONS IN YOUR BODY --
-- UNTIL EVERY CELL IN YOUR BODY IS HARMONICALLY TUNED.
AHHH!
IT FRIGHTENED ME.
I... CAN'T.
CAN'T?
OR WON'T?
YOU ARE AT ONE WITH THE UNIVERSE, MORE THAN MOST HUMANS.
THTHUNK
THE POWERS OF THE VISIONISTIC ARTS ARE ALREADY OPEN TO YOU, BUT YOU MUST CHOOSE TO BECOME ONE WITH THEM. --
-- EMOTIONS ARE THE FIRST DOOR IN. CHOOSE TRUST, JETTA --
-- CHOOSE TRUST.

I WANT TO GO HEAR COMMANDER MYKA WATKINS SPEAK AT THE PAVILION.
HE BROUGHT SOME POLITIA CADETS. I'M GONNA BE A CADET.

COMMANDER WATKINS IS STILL IN ATLAND CITY?
YES. AND I'M GONNA TO MEET HIM.

I THOUGHT THE CORPORATE LEADERS IN SANGELINO DECIDED THE ORBIS TEMPLE ATTACKS WERE A "ROGUE BIODROID MALFUNCTION"?
I KNOW TOO MANY PEOPLE WHO WERE MURDERED THAT DAY TO CALL IT A ROGUE MALFUNCTION.
THE FACT HE'S STILL HERE MUST MEAN SOMETHING.

WATKINS CAN GO BACK TO SANGELINO AND TAKE EVERY BLACKGUARD BIODROID WITH HIM.
...THE BIODROIDS, OUR PROTECTORATE FORCES?
THEY'RE COOL. THEY SAVE PEOPLE!
NOT ANYMORE, RYKER.
THE CO-FEDERATION HAS NEVER CARED BOUT ATLANTIA. THEY PROVED THAT BY NOT SHUTTING DOWN THE BIODROID ROBOTS YEARS AGO.
THEY WOULD IF WE JOINED THE COLLECTIVE.
NO POLITICS TODAY, DAVEL.
NONE.
JETTA -- LOOK!
THEY HAVE THE OUTBACK ARCHERY FINALS TODAY --
-- AND A ZOCCAIR ANTI-GRAVITY KICKOFF.
ARE YOU GONNA ENTER?
...JETTA...?

ATLAND CITY.
THE FUTURE OF THE FUTURE.
THE ATLANTIAN WORLD FAIR
AWESOME!
THIS DOESN'T SUCK.
ALL RIGHT. THIS IS COOLER THAN MY GAME -- SO FAR.
TOLDJA!
I NEED TO GO GET LOST FOR AN HOUR.
AH! SPEAKING OF THAT...
...DAVEL?

HANDS OUT. TAKE THESE!
IF ANYONE GETS SEPARATED, PASS YOUR THUMB THROUGH THE CENTER LIGHT AND IT WILL CONNECT YOU TO MOM AND ME.
THEN JUST STAY PUT --
-- IT WILL GIVE MOM, JETTA, AND ME DIRECTIONS TO YOU, RYKER.
AND REMEMBER, IF THE SYSTEM GOES DOWN, THE PLAN IS --
MEET BACK AT THE VAN, ASAP!
DAD! MOM --
-- WE HAVE TO GO!
ZOCCAIR SHOOT OFF!
THEY ARE OFFERING THE NEW GAMING HAND-HELD AS A PRIZE!

I'M SO SORRY ABOUT JAX, JETTA.
...NO, YOU'RE NOT.
HEY. WANNA TRY YOUR LUCK?
YOU'RE THE BEST AND THE YOUNGEST CENTER REGIONAL CHAMPION ANVIL HIGH EVER HAD.
HE CHEATED ON ME WITH MY BEST FRIEND, MOM.
MY BEST FRIEND!
I LOSE MY TWO BIGGEST RELATIONSHIPS IN ONE BREATH --
-- BUT I'M THE ONE WHO'S TOO SERIOUS?!
PLEASE DON'T GET ALL SPIRITUAL ON ME.
CAN I JUST HAVE AN HOUR TO MYSELF, MOM?
I PROMISE I WILL LET IT GO AFTER THAT. I JUST NEED SOME TO FEEL BAD ABOUT THIS.
WHAT CAN I DO TO HELP YOU BE HERE IN THE MOMENT AND ENJOY THIS?
THIS PAIN WILL BE WAITING FOR YOU WHEN YOU GET HOME. OR NOT. YOUR CHOICE.
SURE. ONE HOUR. WE'LL MEET YOU RIGHT BACK HERE.
DEAL...?
THUMB ON THE BUTTON --
-- AND WE'LL FIND YOU IF YOU CAN'T GET BACK.
PIK-NIK

COME SEE THE TRANSPORTATION OF THE FUTURE.
MOLECULAR PARTICLE TRANSPORT. TRAVEL AROUND THE WORLD IN A FEW SECONDS.
HUNGRY? SEE WHAT IT'S LIKE TO PRINT YOUR DINNER!
...WHAT NOW?
WHERE DO I EVEN START?
GO TO THE MOON IN AN HOUR!
WANT TO TRY A QUICK TRIP?
NOT UNTIL YOU WORK OUT THE BUGS THAT DON'T BRING ALL THE PARTICLES BACK.

YOUNG LADY, SEE WHAT IT'S LIKE TO PRINT YOUR DINNER! ALL ORGANIC.
NOPE. NO THANKS, TRYING TO QUIT.

YOU CAN GROW, PROCESS, AND DESIGN YOUR ENTIRE WARDROBE. THESE FAST-GROWING HEMPS ARE SUSTAINABLE TREES.
YOU CONVERT BOTH LEAVES AND BARK TO FABRIC AND THAT FABRIC CAN BE CONVERTED INTO SMART CLOTH TO MONITOR EXTERIOR AND INTERIOR TEMPERATURE, CHECK YOUR VITALS, AND CONVERT HUMIDITY TO WATER.

THAT'S FOR CLOTHING.
WAIT UNTIL YOU SEE HOW YOU CAN MAKE IT INTO FURNITURE.
NO --
-- JUST... NO.

WHOA -- WHOA!
WHOMP

-:SNIF:-
THEY'RE GONE!
HEY. IT'S OKAY. TAKE A BREATH. WHO'S GONE? WHAT HAPPENED?
MY PARENTS GOT LOST. THEY WERE RIGHT HERE, AND THEN...
HEY. IT'S ALL RIGHT --
-- YOU'RE ALL RIGHT.
WE'LL FIND THEM.
WHAT'S YOUR NAME?
-:SNIF:-
NONR --
-- NONR SEAGATE.
THEY DIDN'T MEAN TO GET LOST!

NO ONE MEANS TO GET LOST. SO NO WORRY.
WE'LL FIND THEM. RIGHT?
YEAH. OKAY.
C'MON. LET'S SEE IF THERE'S A LOST AND FOUND THAT CAN HELP US.
YEOW!
BUMMP!
GOT YOU!
COMMANDER, ARE YOU OKAY?
WATCH WHERE YOU'RE GOING, CIVILIANS!

NO PERMANENT HARM DONE HERE, I TRUST?
I LIKE YOUR UNIFORM!

YOUR BOSS SHOULD WATCH WHERE HE'S GOING.
DO YOU KNOW WHO YOU'RE TALKING ABOUT?

YEAH. ONE MORE POLITIA ELITE WHO DOESN'T CARE ABOUT THE PEOPLE OF ATLANTIA.
STAND DOWN, CADET PETERSON.
THAT'S AN ORDER.

THE YOUNG LADY'S RIGHT. I WASN'T LOOKING.
ARE YOU BOTH OKAY?
OH, SHIT --
MY MOM AND DAD GOT LOST.
-- YOU'RE COMMANDER MYKA WATKINS!
IT'S A PLEASURE TO MEET YOU...?

I'M JETTA A AND THIS IS NONR SEAGATE.
HE GOT SEPARATED FROM HIS PARENTS --
-- AND MY BROTHER IS A CRAZY HUGE FAN OF YOURS.
YOU'RE TOTALLY WRONG ABOUT THE BLACKGUARD ATTACK BEING A FLUKE.
IT WAS SENTIENT, BECAUSE THEY TOTALLY KNEW WHAT THEY WERE DOING WHEN THEY ATTACKED THE ORBIS TEMPLE AND KILLED ALL THOSE PEOPLE AND --

-- AND --
CLAP
CLAP
CLAP
CLAP
CLAP

WHY DON'T ALL OF YOU COME OVER TO THE POLITIA PAVILION AT OH THREE HUNDRED --
-- ESPECIALLY YOU, JETTA --
-- AND JOIN MY TOWN HALL?

WE CAN ALL TALK ABOUT IT --
-- AND MAYBE YOU CAN HELP ATLANTIA MAKE THE CHOICE TO JOIN THE UNITED CO-FEDERATION --
-- SO WE CAN LEGALLY HELP YOU.

IS THERE A PROBLEM, COMMANDER?
NEGATIVE. BIODROIDS DISMISSED.
YOU KNOW...
...THEY'RE NOT SUPPOSED TO TRAVEL IN PAIRS.
AFFIRMATIVE. THANK YOU, JETTA.
THAT WAS A COMMAND --
-- I SAID DISMISSED!
CADET PETERSEN, DO A DIGITAL TRACK AND REPORT THOSE BIODROIDS TO SECURITY.
CADET ANGELA, GET A LOCATION TO THE NEAREST LOST AND FOUND AREA FOR MISS A.
COPY, SIR.
KLIK KLIK
KLIK

AH, HERE WE GO, MISS A...
WOW. THANKS. NICE WRISTSPONDER.
CADET PETERSEN, GIVE MISS A A COUPLE OF PASSES TO THE TOWN HALL.
FOUR.
SIR, WE --
THAT'S A COMMAND, CADET.
SHE SOUNDS LIKE SHE HAS A LOT TO SAY.
YESSIR.
HERE YOU ARE, MA'AM.
THANK YOU, SIR.
MY BROTHER WILL BE ECSTATIC.
COMMANDER, ALL THE BLACK GUARDS ARE ACTING... DIFFERENT.
BEFORE YOU LEAVE US, PLEASE TEST THEIR INDIVIDUAL A.I.
IS THAT AN ORDER, OR A SUGGESTION?
...A HOPE.

BRING UP INDIVIDUAL A.I. TESTING IN THE TOWN HALL.
I LOOK FORWARD TO SEEING YOU AGAIN, MISS JETTA A.

YOU SHOULD CONSIDER JOINING THE POLITIA FORCES.
I'M NOT MUCH OF A FIGHTER.
WE'RE ALL WARRIORS.

THAT HAPPENS WHEN YOU HAVE SOMETHING WORTH FIGHTING FOR.
MY FATHER USED TO SAY, "WHEN FREEDOM IS TAKEN, A WARRIOR IS BORN."
...MINE, TOO.

"A"...? YOU SHOULD GET A WHOLE LAST NAME.
I'LL WORK ON THAT.
NOW, LET'S FIND YOUR PARENTS.

HUNGRY?
SNIFF
SNIFF

OKAY.
ENJOY, KIDDO.
THANKS!
KRUNCH

I DON'T NEED A HEALER.
YOU NEED A SURGEON, AND STITCHES.
WORLD'S FAIR MEDICAL
HMM...
IF I GET STITCHES, I WON'T BE ABLE TO COMPETE THIS AFTERNOON.
IF YOU DON'T GET STITCHES, YOU MIGHT NOT BE ABLE TO EVER SHOOT AGAIN.
SORRY TO KEEP YOU WAITING.
BUT I --
LET ME HELP.
THAT'S... BETTER!
GOOD.
NOW FOLLOW ME.

NAME?
NONR SEAGATE!
TAK TAK TAK
NONANDER HANNIBAL SEAGATE, HUMAN, SEVEN YEARS OLD, BROWN EYES, BLACK HAIR --
-- BORN IN THE TRIBECA REGION, ATLANTIAN OUTBACK.
YOUR PARENTS ARE LOOKING FOR YOU ON THE OTHER SIDE OF THE PAVILION.
YOU'RE VERY LUCKY, YOUNG MAN.
HIS PARENTS HAVE BEEN NOTIFIED AND ARE ON THEIR WAY.
SWEET! HOW'S THAT FOR LUCK? THEY WERE LOOKING FOR YOU, TOO.
IF YOU WANT, MISS, WE CAN TAKE HIM FROM HERE UNTIL THEY ARRIVE.
I'LL WAIT WITH HIM. THANKS.
PARDON ME --

YOU'RE JETTA A...?
I AM.
YOU PLAYED US IN THE ZOCCAIR REGIONAL FINALS TWO YEARS AGO.
YOU WERE AMAZING!
YOU KIDDING?
YOU'RE THE CENTER --
"-- YOU WERE LIKE LIGHTNING ON FIRE!"
"NOT FAST ENOUGH TO STOP YOU, JETTA! THAT LAST FLIP KICK WAS AN IMPRESSIVE MOVE."
IT WAS A TIGHT GAME. FIVE TO SIX.
HEH. I WAS ONLY A SOPHOMORE.
YOU STARRED THAT GAME. DID YOU GET DRAFTED INTO A UNIVERSITY ANYWHERE?
IF YOU WERE THAT GOOD THEN, THE TOP FOUR UNIVERSITIES SHOULD BE OFFERING YOU THE WORLD.

I HAD TO PASS LAST YEAR. STUFF AT HOME. I...
...HAD TO STAY AND HELP MY FAMILY.
YEAH. LIFE IN THE OUTBACK.
MOLECULAR TRANSPORT SYSTEM COMING
PRINTABLE FOODS
MOMMY --
-- LOOK!
WHAT TH --
--THEY'RE NOT ALLOWED TO WALK IN PAIRS.
EVERYBODY KNOWS THAT BUT THEM.
I HEARD THERE'S A PRODUCTION FACILITY IN TEMPLE MOUNTAIN MAKING AN ARMY OF THEM.
GUESS YOU AND I WILL HAVE TO DO SOMETHING ABOUT IT --
-- BEFORE THEY ALL TURN SENTIENT AND WE'RE ALL DEAD.

BY THE WAY. HI --
-- I'M KAI LEE.
"KAI LEE."
YES, I REMEMBER FROM THE FINALS.
SO THAT WOULD MAKE HER YOUR SISTER...
...TANG.
I REMEMBER HER, TOO.
BEST ARCHER IN THE OUTBACK.
I LOST TO TANG -- THREE TIMES!
ZOCCAIR MASTER AND ARCHERY?
NICE TO MEET YOU.
I CAN'T SHOOT FOR THREE WEEKS.
CAN WE GET OUT OF HERE?
T, THIS IS JETTA A.
HE'S MARRIED.
CAN WE GO?
I'M SO NOT MARRIED.
I SHOT YOU MY LIGHT LINE.
CALL ME.

SERIOUSLY?
PING!

WHERE ARE YOU?
WE HAVE TICKETS TO THE IMMERSIVE AV SHOW.
CAN YOU GET HERE IN SIXTY MINUTES?
A MESSAGE. GREAT...
...MISSED THE CALL.

MOM!
DAD!

THAT WAS WAY COOL.
DID YOU FEEL THAT?
NOW WE KNOW EACH OTHER FOREVER.

THEY TOLD ME YOU WATCHED OUT FOR HIM....
THANK YOU!
JETTA A.
HE'S A GREAT KID.
CAN YOU GET HERE?
YOU'VE GOT LESS THAN AN HOUR.
LONG STORY.
YES.
G'BYE, JETTA A.
HOPE YOU GET A WHOLE LAST NAME SOMEDAY!
SENDING YOU OUR LOCATIONS.
ON MY WAY!

OOOPS!
'SCUSE ME...
...PARDON ME...
...COMIN' THROUGH...
K-THOO
YEOW!
-UNNGH-
PiK-NiK Cola

WHAT WAS THAT?
OWW...
LET ME HELP YOU, HONEY...
IS EVERYONE ALL RIGHT?
PLEASE REMAIN CALM.
YEAH. "CALM," SHE SAYS.
...NOTHING.
DAD, AT LEAST I TRIED.
FZZ
MOM! DAD!
ARE YOU OKAY?
CRAP.
BUSTED.

WE ASK THAT ALL VISITORS PLEASE LEAVE THE BUILDING AS CALMLY AS POSSIBLE.
-- JETTA --
ARE YOU -- -- OKAY?!
YES! ARE YOU ALL...
YES --
-- YES. GO TO --
-- VAN.
GOT IT!
TAKE IT EASY.
PLEASE LEAVE THE BUILDING IN AN ORDERLY MANNER.
ONCE OUTSIDE, VOLUNTEERS WILL HAND OUT REENTRY PASSES ONCE WE DETERMINE THE SAFETY OF THE FACILITY.
BE CALM.
I REPEAT, IN AN ORDERLY MANNER.

PLEASE FIND YOUR GROUP AND HEAD TO THE NEAREST EXIT.

SHOW
-GASP-
OW! OWW!!

IMAGINE WHAT YOU NEED, AND IT WILL BE DONE.
MASTA POE --

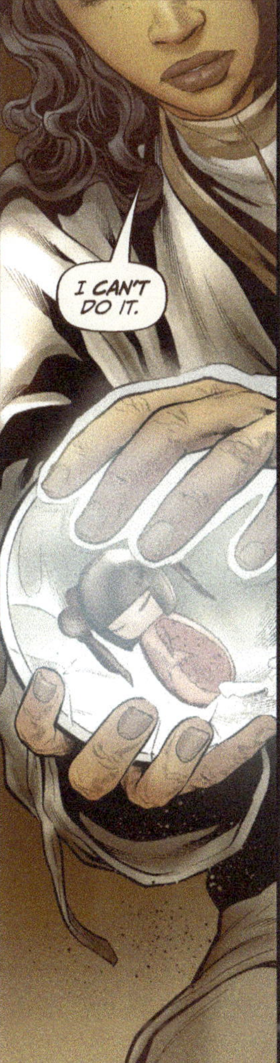

I CAN'T DO IT.

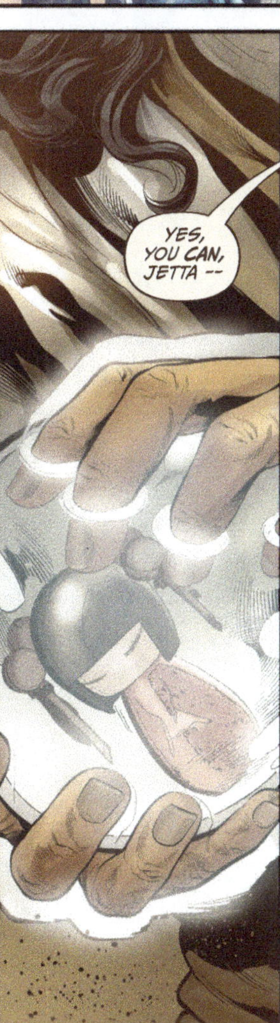

YES, YOU CAN, JETTA --

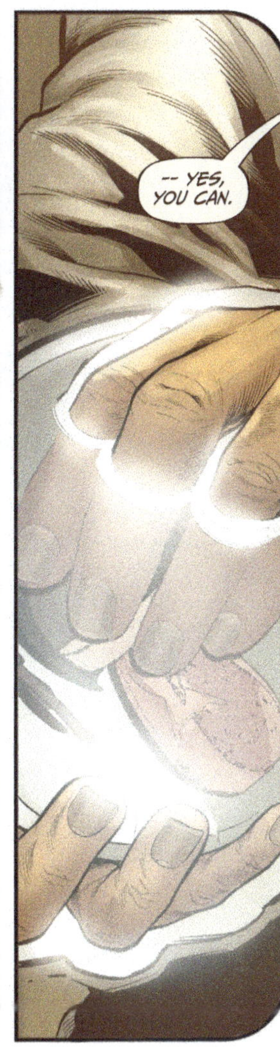

-- YES, YOU CAN.

...YES, YOU CAN...
"...BE CALM."
WHOA--!
UNIVERSAL GOD--!
SOMEONE IS GOING TO GET HURT!
SHOW

MAYBE I CAN DO SOME GOOD HERE....
SHOW
...COME ON...
IT WORKED--!
THANK YOU, MASTA PO.
WHERE'S JAMIE?
RUN FOR COVER!
FIND OUR CAR!
THEY MOVED THE WALL!
LET'S GET OUTTA HERE!
THE WHOLE PLACE IS GONNA BLOW!

THOUGHT I NEVER LEARNED.
I'M GLAD YOU GOT HERE SO FAST!
MASTA POE'S LESSONS PAID OFF!
TIME TO GO, KIDS!

WHRRRRR
ONCE WE'RE SAFELY HOME, WE'LL LOOK INTO REPORTS ABOUT THE EXPLOSION.
RIGHT NOW, I JUST WANT US AS FAR FROM DANGER AS POSSIBLE.
BY THE WAY...
...BEFORE I FORGET --
JETTA --
-- YOU GOT US TICKETS TO SEE THE COMMANDER?!
BEST SISTER EVER!
I'M GONNA NAP. SWITCH ON AUTO PILOT. JOIN ME?
NAH. NOT THE LEAST BIT SLEEPY.
ZZZZZZzzz
WHRRRRR
HEY, SLEEPYHEAD.
LET'S UNPACK THE VAN TOMORROW.
MMMM... I'M GOOD WITH THAT.
HSSSSSS
YOU HAVE ARRIVED HOME. WAKE UP.

I'M STARVING!

JUST BRING IN YOUR LITTLE BAGS FOR NOW.

I'LL HEAD IN AND START DINNER --

VACARY SETTLEMENT

BRATHDOOOM

WHOOOM

WHOOOOM
->UNNGH!<-
OHHH!
WOW!
IS EVERYONE ALL RIGHT? I --
-- OH, NO...
YEOW! MOVE IT, KIDDO!
KROOOM
GET YOUR BROTHER IN THE HOUSE. NOW!
THIS IS ALL WRONG...!
PEACEKEEPERS CAN'T DO THIS!
FWOOOM
I DON'T THINK THEY'RE LISTENING, SQUIRT!
ACKK!
DAVEL!!

I'VE GOT YOU!
WHAT TH--?
BA THOOOM
WE GOTTA GET INSIDE.
-- NO!
THEY'LL BLOW UP THE HOUSE!
LISTEN TO ME.
GET THE KIDS AWAY FROM HERE.
I WON'T LEAVE YOU.

JETTA, TAKE YOUR MOTHER AND BROTHER UP THE BACK HILL PATH WE RUN.
GO TO THE PLATEAU.
YOU SAID NEVER GO IN THERE --!

BRA-THOOOM
MISTER BONDI'S THERE.
TELL HIM IT'S STARTED --
--AND--
--TO--
-- GIVE YOU ALL COORDINATES --
-- TO THE CORE.

TELL HIM...
WHEN FREEDOM IS TAKEN, A WARRIOR IS BORN.
REMEMBER THOSE WORDS?

OWW!
HEY!
MOM? RYKER??

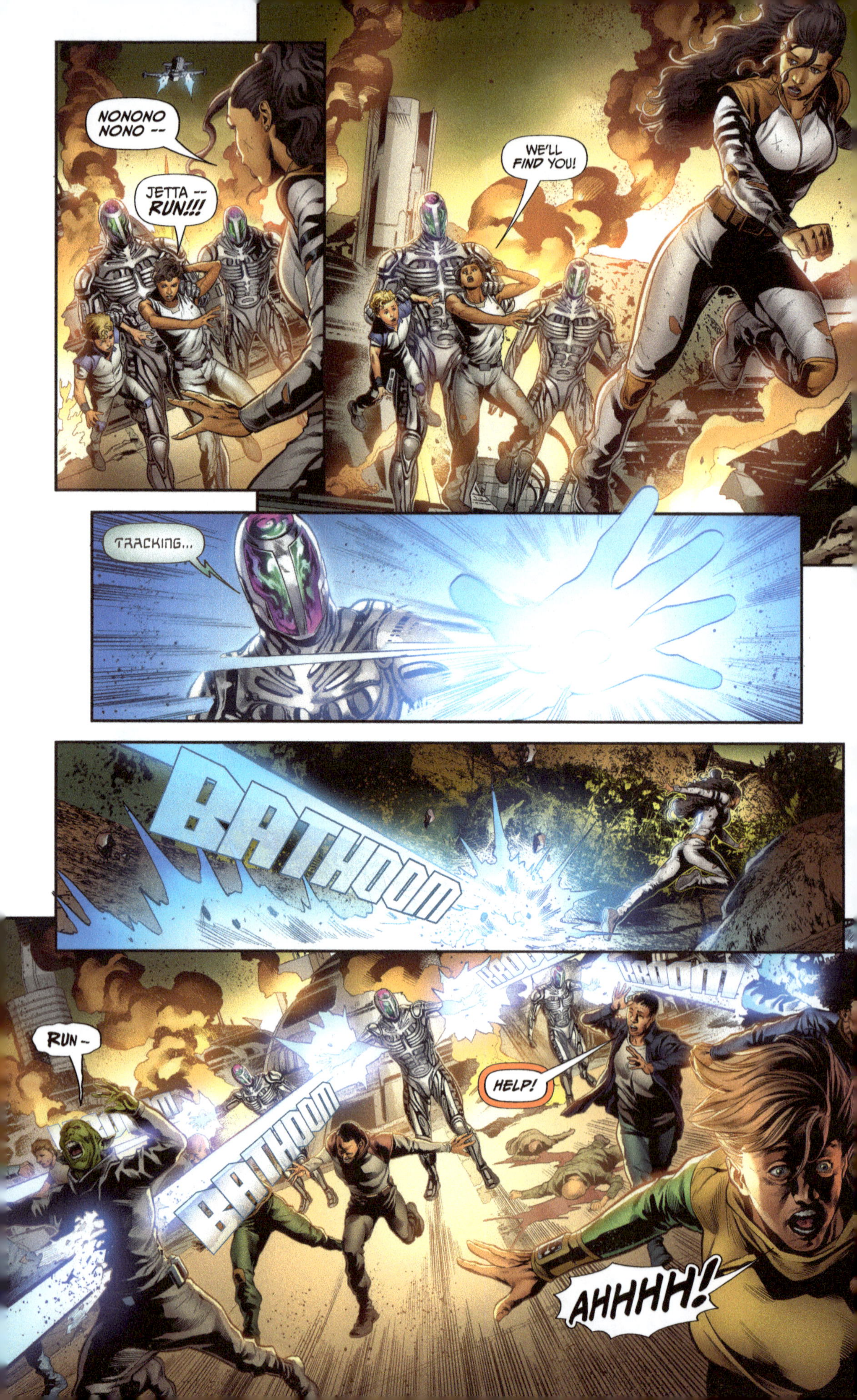

NONONO
NONO --
JETTA --
RUN!!!
WE'LL
FIND YOU!
TRACKING...
BATHOOM
RUN --
BATHOOM
HELP!
AHHHH!

TRACK.
PURSUE.
DESTROY.

AHHH!

SPRUNK
I NEVER BELIEVED THEY WERE PEACEKEEPERS!
P.KOW
P.KOW

I'M GONNA GIVE THEM A PEACE OF MY MIND!

TH-POW

SPRUNK

LET HIM GO!
-UNNGH- NOT -- -- WITHOUT -- -- YOU!
WOW! THANKS, MOM!
MOM!
CAPTURED.
OW! OWW!
LET HER GO!
SECURED.
RYKER-- -- MOM-- -- DAD!
WHOOM
-GASP-
SO MANY PEOPLE -- -- DEAD.

RUN MB
SPRAKK!
TOO CLOSE -- !
KRAKKLE
KRAKK
-:UNNHH:-
LET'S RETURN THE FAVOR!
WHUNK!
KRUNCH
SIGHTED.
PURSUE.

DAD'S THICKET OF BUSHES...?

THE PLACE HE'D TOLD ME --
-- TO STAY AWAY FROM!

KRUNNK
-OOOF-

CREAAAK

KLUNNG

TOK
TOK
TOK

WHRRR

WHRRR

SKRASH
BA-DOOM
TOO CLOSE FOR COMFORT.
RRRIP
~UNNGH!~
SSSSRRRIP
WHRRR
~KOFF~
~KOFF~
KRUMMBL
BLOCKED.
BUT IF I CAN'T GET OUT --
-- THEY CAN'T GET IN.

WHRRR
WHO'S THAT...?
UMM... MISTER BONDI?
MISTER BONDI! IT'S JETTA.
MY FATHER SENT ME!
THE BLACK GUARD ATTACKED US!
THEY KILLED MY FATHER --
-- AND TOOK MY MOTHER AND BROTHER.
WE HAVE TO FIND THEM...
NO. NO! NO!
DON'T BE DEAD.
WE'RE UNDER ATTACK! YOU HAVE TO HELP!!
KLOMMP
NO! NO! NO!!
THIS CAN'T BE HAPPE --

ALERT!
MY SECURITY SENSORS DETECT BLACKGUARD FORCES APPROACHING.
WHOA! WHERE'D YOU COME FROM?
THEY ARE INSIDE THE SECURITY PERIMETER. YOU MUST HIDE!
HELLO! IS ANYBODY THERE? CAN YOU SEE ME? HE'S DEAD.
MISTER BONDI IS DEAD.
PLEASE HELP.
WE'RE UNDER ATTACK.
THE BLACKGUARD KILLED OR CAPTURED EVERYONE.
ANYONE HEARING ME?
MULTIPLE BLACKGUARD READINGS TWENTY METERS FROM WARRIOR ONE.
SKRAP
SKRUMMP
SURVIVAL RECOMMENDATION, GO NEGATIVE IN FIFTEEN SECONDS.
...SOMEONE'S DIGGING US OUT?
HUH?
SHIFT YOUR PARTICLES FROM A POSITIVE STATE TO A NEGATIVE STATE.
I... I DON'T KNOW HOW!
GO NEGATIVE... OR DIE.
WHAT?!

YOU MUST IMPLEMENT THE RECOMMENDED SURVIVAL PROTOCOL IN FIVE... FOUR... THREE...
AHHH!
...TWO... ONE...
SKRASSSH
HUMAN. DECEASED. ONE HOUR.
MARK DNA FOR TRACE AND REPORT.

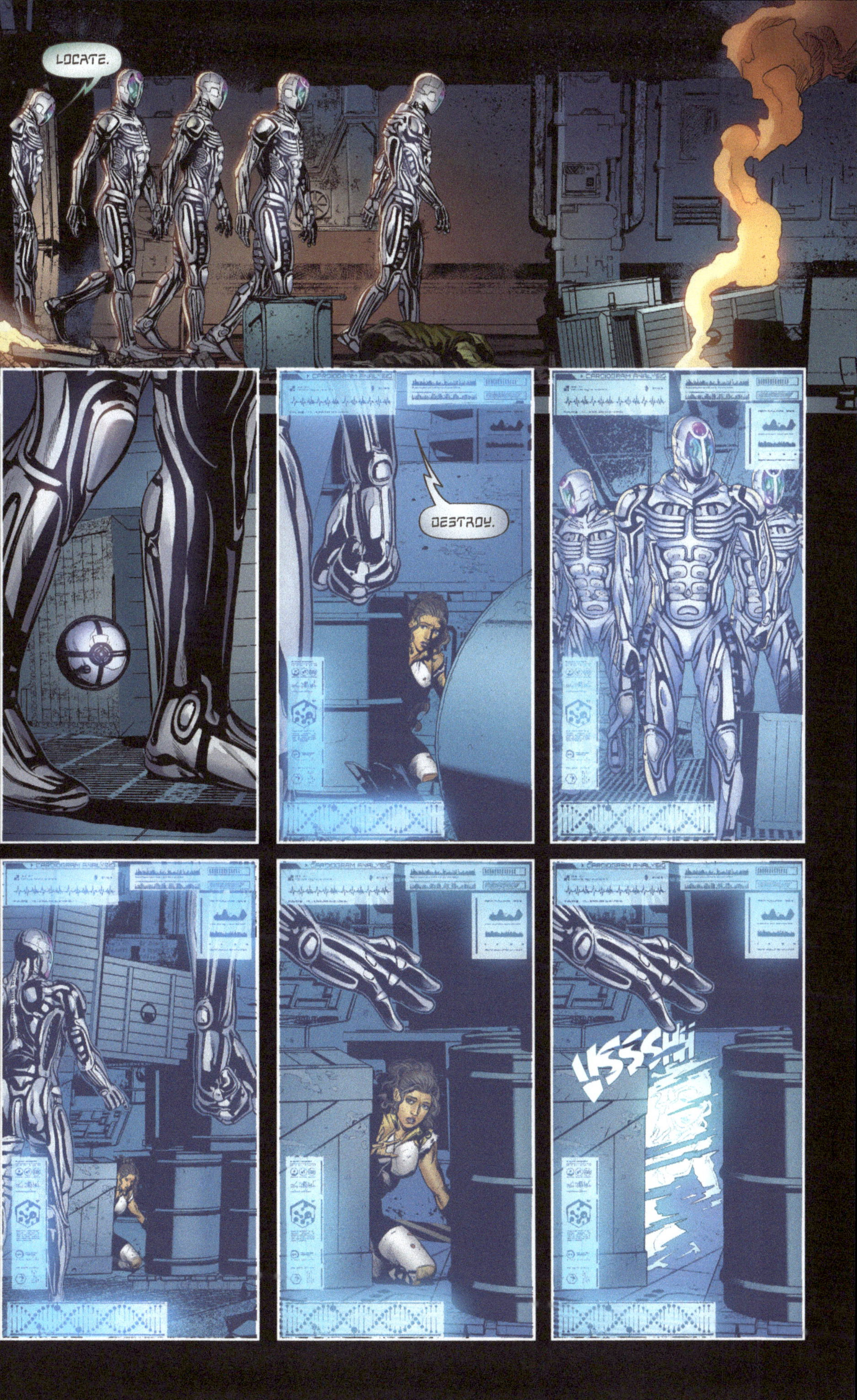

LOCATE.

DESTROY.

KSSSH

ALL LIFE FORCE EXTINGUISHED.
MARK AS CLEAR AND SCHEDULE AREA FOR A FULL FACILITY PURGE.
FTOOM
CEASE SEARCH!
ORDER PARTICALIZATION!
RETURN TO TRANSPORTS.

HRRRR
BLUUURG
OH...
NO --
-- I'M SO SORRY, MISTER BONDI...

WEAPONS!
THEY LOOK PRE-QUAKE.
I SAW THEM IN OLD AUDIO-VISUAL FILES ABOUT THE END OF TIMES CENTURY.
I NEED A BLASTER.
WHRRR
THIS IS A PERSONAL SECURITY BOT.
IT'S OLD.
SHIT.
I THINK YOUR RECEIVER IS DAMAGED.
LET'S GET A BETTER LOOK AT YOU.
MAYBE IF I --
KLIK
KLIK
KLIK

MY NAME IS JETTA A.
IF ANYONE CAN HEAR ME, MISTER BONDI IS DEAD.
THE BLACKGUARD PROTECTORATES --
-- MACHINES DESIGNED AND PROGRAMED TO HELP HUMANS --
-- OUR DEFENDER FORCES --
-- HAVE MALFUNCTIONED, BEEN SABOTAGED, AND BECOME SENTIENT.
THEY HAVE ATTACKED AND DESTROYED THE VACARY SETTLEMENTS.
I'M COMMUNICATING FROM THE FOOTHILLS OUTSIDE OF THE BARAKA SETTLEMENT IN THE NORTHERN ATLANTIA'S OUTBACK.
THEY'VE KILLED OR CAPTURED EVERYONE. MY FATHER IS DEAD AND MY MOTHER AND BROTHER HAVE BEEN TAKEN, ALONG WITH ONLY WOMEN AND CHILDREN.
I DON'T KNOW WHY.
THE RECEIVER ON THIS BOT IS BROKEN --
-- THIS IS THE ONLY TECH THAT DOESN'T RUN ON THE VYBERNET.
FROM THE CODE, MAYBE IT'S THE OLD INTERNET --
-- MAYBE.
I'VE GOT SOME KIND OF SYSTEMS DESK MONITOR. IT'S BROKEN.
AND I DON'T SEE ANY HOLOGRAPHIC OR 3-D MONITORS.

"WARRIOR ONE."
THIS BOT IS CALLED WARRIOR ONE.
THAT MUST HAVE BEEN MISTER BONDI'S CALL NAME.
I THINK THIS OLD, PERSONAL BOT, THE CAMERA, PERIMETER SECURITY, AND EMOTIONAL TRACK SYSTEMS MOSTLY WORK. I THINK.
PLEASE ANSWER.
PLEASE LET ME KNOW YOU'RE OUT THERE, SOMEWHERE, RECEIVING THIS.
PLEASE COME.
KROO
UNIVERSAL GOD--!
-- WHY IS THIS HAPPENING??
THABOO
OH, NO --

THEY'RE PURGING OUR TOWN. THEY'RE KILLING EVERYONE!
WH2Z
"WHY ARE THEY DOING THIS??
"THEY'RE ALL DYING, AND I DON'T KNOW WHAT TO DO."
KABADOOO
NO ONE EVER TAUGHT US HOW TO STOP A REVOLT --
"-- OR QUELL A REVOLUTION FROM MACHINES MADE TO PROTECT US.
"WHOEVER YOU ARE, PLEASE COME.
"HELP US! ANYONE!"

IF YOU CAN HEAR ME, PLEASE COME.
BLIPP
END TRANSMISSION
NINE HOURS LATER:
SADNESS.
SENSORS DETECT HIGH LEVELS OF THE EMOTION SADNESS.
...WHAT?
YOU ARE SAD.
YOU ARE ALSO EXUDING CONFUSION.
YOU BECAME INVISIBLE AND YOU DON'T KNOW HOW. BUT YOU DO.
OH, SO YOU TALK NOW?

MY WORLD JUST SHIFTED INTO A NIGHTMARE.
AND I DON'T KNOW WHAT TO DO.
LIGHTS.
YOU ARE NOT WARRIOR ONE.
WARRIOR ONE IS DEAD.
I AM PROGRAMMED TO TRACK ON WARRIOR ONE.
YOU ARE NOT WARRIOR ONE.
WE ESTABLISHED THAT. REPROGRAM AND TRACK ON MY LIFE FORCE.
NOW TURN ON THE LIGHTS.
ARE NOT WARRIOR ONE!
WARRIOR ONE IS DEAD. REPROGRAM AND TRACK ON ME!
CONFIRM!
CONFIRM!
CONFIRM.
AFFIRMATIVE.

NOW GIVE ME SOME GODDAMN LIGHT!
LIGHTS ON.
GAHHH!!!
OFF! LIGHTS OFF! OFF!
DIM THEM!
DIMMING NOW.
YOU ANSWER TO MY COMMAND ONLY.
YOU GOT THAT? AFFIRMATIVE?
AFFIRMATIVE.
SAY... WHAT'S THAT?
CLARIFY.
THESE. WHAT KIND OF BLASTERS ARE THESE?
NOT BLASTERS.
INSUFFICIENT DATA TO MATCH.

LET'S SEE WHAT ELSE WE CAN FIND.
SORRY, MISTER BONDI.
I CAN GUESS WHAT THESE ARE.
I CAN CONDENSE WATER. HE'S GOT AN OLD I.S. 570.
THIS STUFF IS ANCIENT --
WHAT ELSE CAN I FIND AROUND HERE...?
CLEARLY MISTER BONDI HAD COMPANY MORE MY SIZE AT SOME POINT. I --
I --
BATHOOM

THAT WAS CLOSE!
WHAT'S GOING --
-- ON...?
OH, NONONONO!!
HE WAS RIGGED AND READY FOR A FIGHT.
LET'S SEE IF I FARE ANY BETTER.
NOT THAT IT DID HIM --
-- MUCH GOOD.
~KOF~
~KOF~
YOUR ACTIONS ARE UNNECESSARY AND IMPRACTICAL.
WARRIOR ONE SHOWS NO VITAL SIGNS.
HE'S DEAD.
CONFIRMED.
THEN SHUT UP AND GET THE HELL OUT OF MY WAY!

I NEED THESE SUPPLIES.
WARRIOR ONE. I DETECT YOUR THREAT LEVEL ACCELERATING.
MULTIPLE PEACEKEEPERS APPROACHING.

I READ TWO --
-- NO --
-- THREE TRANSPORTS...
...THIRTY METERS OUT.
HOSTILE.
THUMP

THIS IS ILLOGICAL.
WARRIOR ONE IS DEAD.
LISTEN --

-- I CAN'T LEAVE HIM HERE.
YOU NEED SUPPLIES.
THREAT LEVEL...
CLANNG

BATHOOM
KRAKOOOM
-UNGH-
OOOOF!
-HUFF-
-HUFF-
BUMMP
BUMMP
BDUMMB
BDOOOM
-WHEW!-
THEY ARE TEN METERS AWAY AND CLOSING.
YOU LEFT ME.
I'LL LEAVE YOU AGAIN IF YOU DON'T PAY ATTENTION AND LISTEN.
WHRRRR
FOLLOW ME.

~UNGH~
WHY DON'T YOU GROW A PAIR --
-- OF HELPFUL HANDS --?
I AM NOT FITTED WITH MOLECULAR MICRO FABRICATION CAPABILITIES.
THEREFORE, I CANNOT COMPLY.
BUMP
BUMP
OW!
BUMP
KATHOOM
KATHOOM
KATHOOM
WHOOM
YOU MUST SHIELD.
NOW.

SUCCESSFUL.
BUT MISCALCULATED.
WHAT ARE YOU DOING OUT--?
NEVER MIND.
BOT -- HERE -- NOW!
CARDIOGRAM ANALYSIS
CARDIOGRAM ANALYSIS

NEVER MIND.
BOT -- HERE -- NOW!
CARDIOGRAM ANALYSIS

BOOOM

KRAKOOOM

KRAKA
DOOOM

BA DA THOOM

BA BA DOOM

STAY FOCUSED, JETTA...
...CHOOSE COURAGE!!

~HUFF~
I --
-- NEVER BURIED ANYONE, BEFORE...
WHRRRR
FLUPP
...I DON'T HAVE A COMMUNICATOR TO SAY NOBLE WORDS ABOUT YOUR LIFE, MISTER BONDI...
...OR A ROCKET TO SEND YOUR SPIRIT BACK INTO THE COLLECTIVE SOURCE POWER OF THE UNIVERSAL GOD.
JUST THIS:
YOU SAVED MY LIFE.
EVEN DECEASED, YOU GAVE ME SHELTER...
...FOOD AND WATER...
...AND THESE WEAPONS I DON'T UNDERSTAND YET.
I'M SORRY YOU HAD TO DIE.
KCHOK

I DIDN'T KNOW YOU WELL. I SAW YOU AT THE DOME AND WATCHED YOU STAND AND LISTEN --
-- AS WE SANG AND OFFERED COLLECTIVE THOUGHTS IMAGINING A BETTER WORLD INTO BEING.
I DON'T REMEMBER THAT YOU EVER SHARED ANYTHING, ONLY THAT YOU KEPT WATCH OVER US ALL.
I DON'T KNOW IF YOU HAD A FAMILY BUT, IF YOU DID, THEY WOULD BE PROUD OF HOW PREPARED YOU WERE --
-- TO FIGHT THESE BIODROIDS WHO TOOK SO MANY OF OUR FRIENDS. THEY TOOK MY MOTHER AND MY BROTHER.
YOU SAW IT COMING.
I PROMISE ON YOUR LIFE, I'LL FIND A WAY TO STOP THE BLACK GUARD AND GET MY MOTHER AND BROTHER BACK.

I AM GRATEFUL FOR YOU, AND I'LL ALWAYS REMEMBER THAT I'M ALIVE BECAUSE OF YOU, MISTER BONDI.
THANK YOU.
GO IN LIGHT.
WHRRRR

THIS IS JETTA A, SIGNING IN AS WARRIOR ONE.
I DON'T KNOW WHO YOU ARE OR IF ANYONE IS EVEN OUT THERE RECEIVING THESE FEEDS --
-- BUT IF YOU CAN TRACK ME, I WILL BE HEADING SOUTH THROUGH THE VALLEY PATHS...
...ON FOOT.
THESE WEAPONS ARE OLD, AND I DON'T KNOW HOW POWERFUL THEY ARE OR IF THEY CAN TAKE ON A BLASTER, BUT --
-- MAYBE...
...IF I'M LUCKY...
...THEY CAN DAMAGE A FEW PEACEKEEPERS AND SHUT DOWN SOME BLACKGUARDS.
MAYBE.
THIS IS WARRIOR ONE, SIGNING OFF.
WAVEFORM ANALYSIS
YOU ARE UNDER OBSERVATION.
BOT, GIVE ME AN ENERGY READ OF THE AREA.
WAVEFORM ANALYSIS
...HUMAN...?
...BLACKGUARD MACHINES?
SPLICER.
...FRIENDLY?
HUNGRY.

UH-OH.
SNAPP
FIT! FIT!
IT'S NOT WORKING!
KAKLAK
ANOTHER CLIP--?
KLIK
YES!
GOING NEGATIVE IS NOT AN OPTION.
ROARRRR
KRAAKK

AHHHHH!
BRATATATATATATAT
THOP
THOP
THOP
THOP
THOP
SPLATT
THUNK
WARRIOR ONE!
WARRIOR ONE!

WARRIOR ONE!
IT'S NO USE...
...WE HAVE TO HELP HER.
TRANSMIT!
TELL HER WHO WE ARE -- WHERE WE ARE, INSIDE THIS MOUNTAIN.
BONDI GAVE HER WARRIOR ONE. SHE NEEDS TO GET THAT BOT AND HERSELF TO THE CORE!
WE CAN'T TRANSMIT!
HAVE YOU CONNECTED WITH COMMANDER MYKA? FIND HIM --
-- HELP THIS GIRL!
WE CAN'T RISK IT. THE COMMANDER AND HIS CADETS ARE PINNED DOWN IN ATLAND CITY!
SHE HAS TO DO IT. SHE'S WARRIOR ONE!

"...SHE'S JUST GOT TO GET HERE. ALL OF THEM JUST HAVE TO GET HERE."
YOU PICKED ONE HELLUVA TIME TO NAP.
GLITCHING ON ME ISN'T HELPFUL.
LET ME CLEAN YOU UP SO YOU CAN SEE.
CARDIOGRAM ANALYSIS
WHAT SPLICER BREED IS THIS?
PROTIUS ONE -- PART CANINE, REPTILIAN AND SYNTHETIC GENETICS.
WEIGHT APPROXIMATELY TWO-HUNDRED EIGHTY-FOUR KILOS... ...NO LIFE DETECTED.
I'M NOT THE ONLY ONE WHO SHOT THIS THING.
LOOK AT THESE ARROWS IN ITS BACK.
TUNGSTEN ALLOY, FREQUENTLY USED FOR COMPETITIVE --
WHRRRR
THAT'S A KID SCREAMING!!
MAYBE RYKER'S ALIVE!
AAAAAAHHHH
ALERT! BLACKGUARDS APPROACHING. EIGHT HUNDRED METERS.
WHAT'S THAT?
TRAVEL VAN. ASSAULTED AND DOWNED BY PEACEKEEPER WEAPONS.
WHRRRRR

WHRRRR
...ANY SURVIVORS?
POSSIBLY.
BLOOD TRAIL INDICATES BODIES WERE IN MOTION.
CANNOT FOLLOW HEAT SIGNATURES BECAUSE VEHICLE IS ON FIRE.
FIRE? I DON'T SEE ANY --
IT IS NOT BURNING ON A SPECTRUM VISIBLE TO HUMANS.
NOR IS THERE SMOKE OR MUCH AMBIENT HEAT.
HOW COULD THAT --
FWOOOSH!
YEOW!
TWHRRR

AYEEIH!
THAT CRY AGAIN!
WARRIOR ONE! HURRY!

YOU SHOULD HAVE GONE NEGATIVE.
UNIVERSAL GOD!
THWIP
THUNK

FIVE METERS THAT WAY.
WHO -- ?
THUPP
KAI LEE?!
TANG?
NONR?
HEY, JETTA.
TOO LATE FOR THE RESCUE.
WHAT ARE YOU DOING HERE?
-SNIF-
-SNIF-
...JETTA A??
YOU SHOT AT ME! WHAT THE...??
YOU'RE DANGEROUS. YOU HAVE WEAPONS. I DON'T LIKE YOU. PICK ONE.
SAVE IT FOR THE WAR OR END IT HERE, TANG!
I ONLY MISSED BECAUSE I'M WOUNDED.
LADIES, PLEASE --
-- THIS IS ABOUT NONR.
HIS FOLKS SHIELDED HIM WITH THEIR OWN BODIES. WE DID ALL WE COULD.
NONR, WHAT DID --

WARRIOR ONE --
-- BLACKGUARD ATTACK IMMINENT.
WE GOTTA MOVE OUT!!!
BATHOOOMM
GRIOT!!
GET 'EM WHERE IT HURTS!
DO THEY HURT ANYWHERE?
YOU CAN SHORT-CIRCUIT THEM IN THE EYE BANDS, BUT --
PCHOW
PCHOW
PCHOW
PCHOW
THWIPP
DON'T MIND IF I DO!
BRZZT
THUPP
GOT 'EM!

YOU DON'T SUCK AS BAD AS I THOUGHT.
SHUT UP, TANG.
WHERE'S NONR?!
KRUMMP
I'M HERE, JETTA A. I GOTTA GET TO MY GRANDPARENTS.
GRIOT KNOWS THE WAY, BUT SHE'S HURT, AND CAN'T FLY."
WE'LL GET YOU THERE. I PROMISE.
BOT, SEND A HELP SIGNAL!
AND I PROMISE I'LL FIND YOU A LAST NAME.
COMMANDER, ARE YOU GETTING THIS PRIORITY DISTRESS CALL?
WHO THE HELL...?!
PCHOW
PCHOW
PCHOW
PCHOW
AHHH!
PCHOW

JETTA! IT'S COMMANDER MYKA.
HOW ARE YOU ON A POLITIA COMM FEED? WHERE ARE YOU?
THE OUTBACK!
VACARY SETTLEMENTS. I'M WITH...
...FRIENDS. WE'RE FIGHTING THE BLACKGUARD. CAN YOU COME? PLEASE.
WE'RE PINNED DOWN IN ATLAND CITY. CAN YOU --
-- GET TO THE CORE ICE MOUNTAINS! WE'LL MEET YOU IF WE CAN --
THE BLACKGUARD ARE EVERYWHERE.
KILL THEM OR THEY'LL KILL YOU, JETTA. DO YOU UNDERSTAND?
FIND A REASON WORTH FIGHTING FOR.
THEY KILLED MY FATHER AND TOOK MY MOTHER AND BROTHER.
I HAVE A REASON.
WE ALL DO.
NOW I UNDERSTAND MY FATHER'S WORDS.
"WHEN FREEDOM IS TAKEN, A WARRIOR IS BORN."
END BOOK ONE

WARRIOR ONE™

is based on the world of

THE VISION QUEST

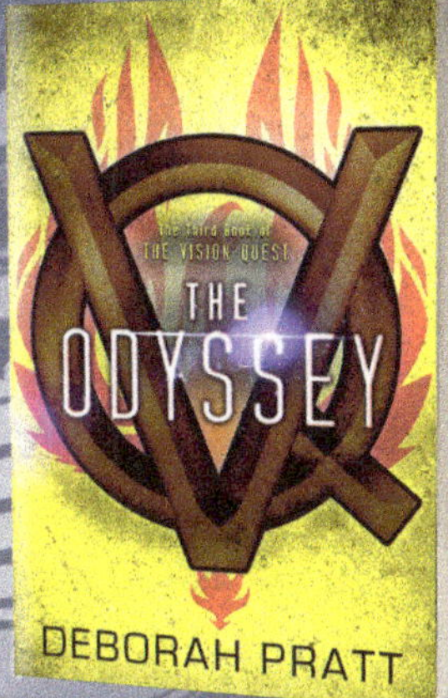

BOOK 5

In the heart-pounding fifth installment of the Vision Quest series, Lazer returns to Atlantia, reuniting with allies Cashton and Kyla to join forces with the formidable Warrior One, Jetta A.

As the relentless war unfolds, they uncover the underground stronghold of the sinister biodroid leader, Five, holding captive Elana Blue and her father, Covax. Covax, the creator of Five's A.I. program, who needs the lost code to stop Five's world-conquering ambitions.

The clock ticks, urging humanity to embrace the Visionistic Arts and unite against Five's impending domination.

Amidst complex relationships and personal struggles, Lazer must confront the truth about his connection to the Blue Gnorb to unlock its powers and thwart Five's deadly plan.

The fate of Atlantia and the world rests on the shoulders of Lazer, Kyla, Cashton, Riana, Jetta A, Masta Poe, and their allies as they race against time to discover the final key to the vision quest and to save everything they hold dear from the clutches of Five and his malevolent forces.

COMING SOON

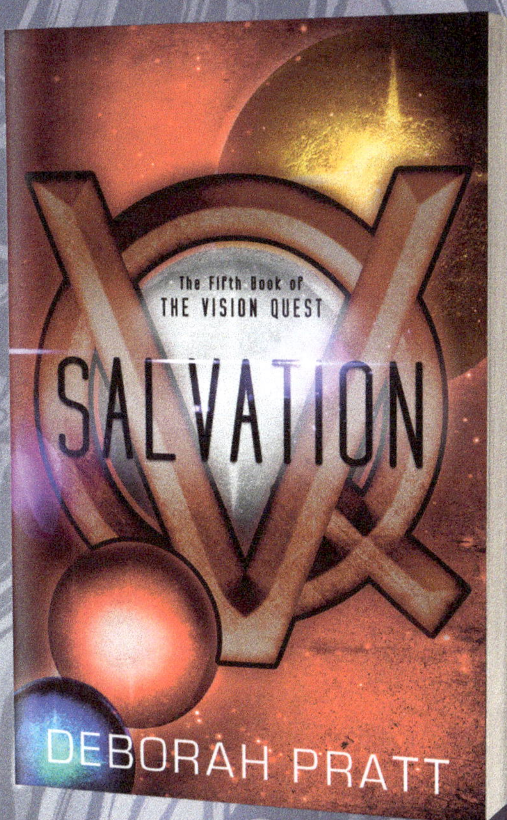

DEBORAH M. PRATT
Creator and Author

A graduate of Webster University with degrees in Psychology and Theatre, Deborah Pratt kicked her career off by winning a nationwide talent search. This achievement brought her from Chicago to Hollywood under contract with NBC. She performed on variety TV shows, played Las Vegas, wrote music and lyrics, sang on multiple albums, and began acting, writing, directing, and producing in theater, television, and film.

Deborah is recognized as the first African-American drama and science-fiction Executive Producer for television. She co-created the NBC series *Quantum Leap* writing 25 episodes of the iconic TV show. Deborah is back as Executive Producer and Director for the new season of the Quantum Leap reboot, airing on NBC and Peacock. She was Co-Executive Producer and Head Writer for *Tequila and Bonetti* on CBS and Co-creator and Executive Producer for *The Net* TV series on USA Network, and directed the *Grey's Anatomy* season 19 finale.

Deborah is an award-winning graduate of AFI/DWW, the American Film Institute's Directing Workshop for Women, making her directorial debut with the film *Cora Unashamed* for Masterpiece Theatre's The American Collection for the BBC and PBS. She graduated from the Fox/AFI/20th Century Fox's Female Feature Film Directors' Initiative. Deborah is a five-time Emmy Award nominee and recipient of The Lillian Gish Award for Women in Film, the Golden Block Award, and various festival awards.

As a published novelist, Deborah breaks the mold of science fiction, creating a science fantasy genre with her soul-bending tale of a future Earth and the key to human empowerment, called *The Vision Quest*. The five-volume series is available on Amazon.com, and she invites you to join her to explore the growing franchise at thevisionquest.com. The Vision Quest universe is the foundation of the *Warrior One* graphic novel story. She invites you to join her at WarriorOneWorld.com.

Deborah fights for women's and minority rights in all walks of life. She lives in Los Angeles, and has two children, Troian and Nicholas-Dante Bellisario. Always seeking to expand her creative horizons in the arts, Warrior One is Deborah's first graphic novel. Deborah M. Pratt is a member of the Television Academy. Directors Guild of America, Screen Actors Guild, Producers Guild of America, and the Writers Guild of America, where she is a former member of the Board of Directors.

WILL CONRAD
Artist

Will Conrad (Vilmar Conrado) was born in Brazil and has been working for the international comics market since the late '90s, when he became an inker for Dark Horse Comics. Before long he developed his storytelling and drawing skills, finding work as illustrator on top titles at Marvel, DC, and Dark Horse. Will is known for his work on *Action Comics, Angel and Faith, Birds of Prey, Black Panther, Buffy the Vampire Slayer, Cyborg, Elektra, Excalibur, Justice League, Kull, New Avengers, Nightwing, Outsiders, Red Sonja, Serenity, She-Hulk, Star Wars, Superman, Wolverine, X-Men, X-23*, and more.

He's most recently been drawing his creator-owned series *Out* and *Red Border* for AWA Studios. Will currently lives in Belo Horizonte, Brazil, with his wife Isabella and his daughters Alice and Leticia.

DAVID CAMPITI
Editor/Adapter

David Campiti's writing career began shortly after graduation from West Liberty University with a degree in Communications. He first worked in radio, both on the air and as a writer/voice artist/producer of humorous radio commercials, then was copy chief for L.G. Balfour Company, the class ring and awards company. He began writing comics, including DC's *Superman*, before packaging comics for a variety of clients. David was founder/editor-in-chief/publisher of Innovation, best known for its graphic novels adapting such books as Anne Rice's *The Vampire Lestat* and Terry Pratchett's *On a Pale Horse*. David edited and published such TV/film tie-in comics as *Beauty and the Beast, Dark Shadows, Lost in Space*, and *Quantum Leap.*

After years behind the publisher desk, David became CEO of Glass House Graphics, an agency/studio producing thousands of pages of story and art each year for Marvel, DC, Dark Horse, Simon & Schuster, and others. His company soon expanded into Glass House Studios, providing animation work on films and TV shows as well as visual effects for live-action. David continues to write, most recently a series of *Goddess Girls, Heroes in Training,* and *Moon Base Alpha* graphic novels for Simon & Schuster. He lives in Orlando, FL with his wife Meryl, daughter Jasmine, and Maltipoo Genie.

CANDICE HAN
Colorist

Candice Han is a professional comic colorist and painter living in Malaysia. She worked with clients including Dark Horse Comics, Disney Publishing Worldwide, Activision, IDW Publishing, Heavy Metal Magazine, Dynamite Entertainment, Valiant Comics, and Ablaze Publishing. She was best known for her work on *Alien: The Original Screenplay* series for Dark Horse Comics. Additionally, her works include *Fancy Nancy* Series, *Call of Duty: Black Ops 4 Digital Comics, Star Trek: Hell's Mirror, Transformers/Back to Future, Wreckers, Savage Circus,* and *Evil Ernie 2021.*

Her colors always spice up your meals.

KATHRYN S. RENTA
Letterer/Editor/Graphic Designer

Kathryn S. Renta is an award-winning artist and 2021 Ringo Award nominated, creative team member for Best Non-fiction Comic Work on *We'll Soon Be Home Again* (Dark Horse). Her production work on the *Heroes Among Us* campaign for Marvel & Adidas expanded to lettering, retouching, compositing, digital asset management, and prepress. This facilitated a smooth delivery for the project to make its premiere at the Adidas flagship store on Times Square in 2019.

In addition to 25 years as a graphic artist, her career includes 20 years in the comic book industry. She has worked on projects for ABDO, Adidas, Activision, Dark Horse Comics, DC Comics, Dynamite Entertainment, Marvel, Viz Media, Allan Amato, Rafael Navarro, and numerous other independent contractors and creators.

ARCT
OCEA
NORTH
ATLANTIC
OCEAN
GUILIANI
MOUNTAINS
TEMPLE
MOUNTAINS
SANGELINO
UNITED CO
FEDERATION
BARAKA
SETTLEMENTS
SHOOTING
FALLS
VACARY
SETTLEMENTS
ATLANTIA
TERRITORIES
NORTH
PACIFIC
OCEAN
ORBIS
JOINT COM
SHINOBA
BAY
ATLAND
CITY
ATLANTIAN STRAIGHTS
PANAZIA
SOUTH
PACIFIC
OCEAN
SOUTH
ATLANTIC
OCEAN
AN

www.ingramcontent.com/pod-product-compliance
Lightning Source LLC
Chambersburg PA
CBHW041205100726
47911CB00016B/870